Please Don't Make Fun of Me

Written by Rachel Chronister

Illustrated by Galih Winduadi

ISBN

978-1-7379851-0-5 Hardback
978-1-7379851-1-2 Paperback
978-1-7379851-2-9 E book

Library of Congress Control Number: 2021918269

Ref:MSG0751337_2l29k4hhXvXOY44DsPg5

Summary: Tommy is scared to start his first day at a new school. He experiences being made fun of and being left out by several students. He encounters a horrible day until "ONE BOY" finally stands up for him and changes his world. This book teaches the Power of One. One student can make a difference. This is a book on kindness, empathy, being a leader, compassion, and forgiveness.

Printed in the U.S.A.
First Edition printed 10/21
Written by: Rachel Chronister
Illustrated by: Galih Winduadi

From the Author

I dedicate this book to all those students who have been left out or have been made fun of and to those students who are willing to be "THE ONE" who stands up for the student being hurt. I have been an educator for 34 years, and as an elementary counselor I told this story many times. The teachers and the students loved this story and would ask me to share it each year. I would show the picture of Tommy on the last page of this book. The students would often gasp when they saw Tommy's picture being wadded up each time a hurtful thing was said or done to him. He soon looked like trash, rippled, shattered, and torn. We would try to straighten out the picture of Tommy but the scars were still there. I decided to put this lesson in a book so many children would be reminded that our words and actions hurt others and can last a lifetime. In this story, because of the courage of just "ONE BOY" that stands up for Tommy, his world changed forever. This book reveals the importance of standing up for a student who is being teased. My goal is for students to show more kindness after reading this book. I live in Owasso, Oklahoma. My husband and I have two grown married children and two wonderful grandchildren, Cooper Reed, who is seven and Collins Tyler, who is three years old and two more grandchildren on the way. We share our home with a red goldendoodle named Marley.

Why do some kids have to be so mean?
Why do they have to make fun of others?
Why do they purposely leave some kids out?
Why do they have to make fun of someone who wears
glasses or make fun of someone who stutters?
Why?

Tommy was all alone and scared. He had to move to Oklahoma from Texas to live with his Aunt Bessie and Uncle Bob whom he had never met. Eight-year-old Tommy carried his battered suitcase off the plane; he was hungry, tired, and scared. Tommy had so many frightening thoughts running through his head. What if Aunt Bessie and Uncle Bob did not come pick him up at the airport? What if they did not really want him to stay with them? What if they are mean people? What if???

All at once Tommy heard someone yelling his name. "Tommy Allbright." The kind looking lady held a sign that said, "Welcome Tommy." He gave her a small hand wave and walked over to her. She gave him a quick hug and said, "Hi Tommy", I am your Aunt Bessie, and this is your Uncle Bob. Uncle Bob reached out to shake Tommy's hand. "We are so glad that you are coming to stay with us. How was your flight? You are so brave to fly all by yourself, Tommy." Aunt Bessie put her arm around him and said, "I know you must be very tired so let's get you home and get you fed."

They drove from the airport to their house. Tommy looked out the window where everything looked so different; it all felt so scary. He was in a car with people he didn't even know, and he missed his mom and dad. Why did he have to leave his family?

They finally arrived at Aunt Bessie and Uncle Bob's house. It was a simple plain house with two bedrooms. Aunt Bessie showed Tommy to his room. It had blue walls, a small bed with blue and white checked bedspread, small dresser, closet, with one shelf hanging over his bed. There was a picture on the wall of a small boy Tommy's age holding a stuffed dog. In his suitcase, he brought his old brown bear that he had since he was one year old. Aunt Bessie came in his room and said, "Let's get some food in that tummy." He had not eaten since 8:00 that morning.

Aunt Bessie made a wonderful hot meal of roast beef, potatoes, carrots, and brownies for dessert. The family bowed their head and said a prayer and Uncle Bob said he was thankful Tommy had come to their home. It made Tommy feel a bit better. Maybe it wouldn't be so bad living here after all. At the end of the meal, Aunt Bessie said, "You know you will have to go to school Wednesday." Tommy looked up at her with tears in his eyes, "Please, please don't make me go to school." Big giant tears rolled down his cheeks. Aunt Bessie tried to console Tommy, "I know you will love school if you just give it a chance Tommy. I am sorry but you have to go to school."

The next morning, she went in to wake him. "Good morning, Tommy," she said, "I made some delicious blueberry pancakes." Tommy sat down to the stack of pancakes. The pancakes and bacon smelled so good! Tommy rubbed his eyes and took a small bite. He did not intend on eating the entire stack of pancakes, but he had never tasted anything so good in his whole life. Aunt Bessie sure knew how to cook great meals! His mom never had the time to cook hot meals.

Aunt Bessie sat Tommy down in the living room and reminded him that they were going to get his hair cut and go to Budget Discount to buy a couple of things for school.   Tears started to wallow up in his eyes. He just could not hold them back. When she opened the suitcase, she saw Tommy only had two pairs of jeans, two shirts, and an old worn sweatshirt that had holes on both elbows. It was pretty much all he owned.

As Tommy and Aunt Bessie got in the car, Aunt Bessie said, "Now, next stop is Budget Discount Store. Tommy carried his bag out as proud as a peacock. He didn't even mind that it was raining. He couldn't remember the last time he had anything new to wear.

As they got in the car, Aunt Bessie said, "We should drive by your new school." Tommy immediately got knots in his stomach, big knots. He slid down in his seat and did not say a word. Aunt Bessie looked at him and said, "I know you don't want to go to school, but Tommy you have to think positive. It is a great school with wonderful teachers, and I know you will make good friends if you just give it a chance." The rain had stopped, and the sun was out. "There is your new school, Tommy." He turned his head and looked but did not say a word. Then he saw some boys playing basketball. He loved basketball, but he still did not want to go to a new school.

As they got in the car, Aunt Bessie said, "We should drive by your new school." Tommy immediately got knots in his stomach, big knots. He slid down in his seat and did not say a word. Aunt Bessie looked at him and said, "I know you don't want to go to school, but Tommy you have to think positive. It is a great school with wonderful teachers, and I know you will make good friends if you just give it a chance." The rain had stopped, and the sun was out. "There is your new school, Tommy." He turned his head and looked but did not say a word. Then he saw some boys playing basketball. He loved basketball, but he still did not want to go to a new school.

The next morning, Aunt Bessie woke him extra early so he would have plenty of time to eat breakfast and get dressed. Tommy brushed his teeth and used Uncle Bob's hair wax. Aunt Bessie said, "Have a great day, Tommy." She gave him a hug as he ran out the door. Tommy was beginning to feel sick as he looked down the road waiting on the bus.

Tommy was beginning to feel sick as he saw the yellow bus come around the curve; it was almost at their driveway. He swallowed hard trying not to feel all the emotions he was feeling. The bus stopped with its flashing red lights right in front of his house. The door opened and the driver yelled out. "Hey, you the new kid I am supposed to pick up?" Tommy let out a sigh and said, "Yes, I guess." "Well, come on, we don't have all morning. Please hurry and find a seat." Tommy felt sick as he started walking to the back of the bus.

He asked one boy if he could sit beside him, but the boy just snickered and said, "No, I have it saved for my friend." Tommy went down a few more rows but no one would scoot over. Finally, as he was nearing the back rows, the bus driver looked in the mirror and yelled, "Would someone please scoot over for the new kid!" In the last seat of the bus sat a kid on the aisle who rolled his eyes and slowly scooted over. The kid kept his headphones on, and he never even acknowledged him. Tommy felt so insignificant, like he was a nobody. He felt all alone! Why couldn't at least one student scoot over for him?

As they pulled up to the school, Tommy saw through the window a man waving at kids as they went into the building. He looked like a nice man and had a big smile on his face and was talking to the kids. It looked like a nice school with a big sign above the front double doors that said, "Welcome to Sunnyside Elementary." He decided he was going to think positive and maybe this school wouldn't be so bad after all.

A teacher spotted Tommy and knew he was new. She introduced herself as the school counselor and asked him his name. She walked him into the school principal's office, "Good Morning, Mr. DoRight, we have a new student today. This is Tommy Allbright." Mr. DoRight stood and shook Tommy's hand and said, "Welcome to Sunnyside, we are glad you are here."

"Tommy, where was your last school?" For the life of him, he could not think of the name of his old school. Finally, Tommy said, "Somewhere in Texas." Principal DoRight said, "Oh my! That is a long way from here. Well, we are so glad you are here at Sunnyside Elementary, and we are going to get you in a great class. Hum, let's see, yes, Mrs. Smith will be your teacher."

Then Ms. Chronister walked Tommy down two flights of stairs and turned down a long hallway. "Here we go Tommy, this is your classroom." Good Morning Mrs. Smith. This is your new student, Tommy Allbright. He came all the way from Texas, and he flew on the airplane by himself to stay with his aunt and uncle. I think that is pretty brave and courageous of Tommy, don't you think Mrs. Smith?" "I sure do!" replied Mrs. Smith. The counselor, Mrs. Chronister got down on Tommy's level and said, "Tommy, if you need anything you come find me, you hear? I will be back in the morning to check on you."

Mrs. Smith said, "Class, we have a new student today. Let's welcome our new student. Would you like to introduce yourself Tommy?" Tommy was scared to make eye contact with any of the students and he struggled to say his name. After stuttering several times, he finally got out "T-o-m-m-y A-l-l-b-r-i-g-h-t." A few students waved "hi," but he saw two boys in the back of the room snickering. Mrs. Smith showed Tommy a seat right behind Sammy Stafford. Tommy slid into his seat and Sam turned around and whispered under his breath. "Nice glasses, "four eyes," are those shoes from Goodwill?" Tommy ignored Sam's mean words, but they stung into his heart. The words cut right through him. He could not help that he had to wear glasses. Why couldn't the kids at least give him a chance?

Finally, it was recess time. Everyone hustled outside, but no one asked Tommy to play. He stood against the wall. Mrs. Smith walked over to Tommy and said, "Hey, let's go play some soccer." She asked Aiden Miller to be his buddy and play with him. Aiden said, "Yes ma'am." But as soon as she turned her back, Aiden said to Tommy, "You aren't good enough to play soccer with us. Go play somewhere else."

When the bell rang, all the kids lined up to go inside. Tommy picked up the water bottle the boy in front of him had dropped and smiled as he handed it to him. When they got back to class, they played "Around the World." Tommy got the hardest word in the whole game. Tommy stuttered as he tried to repeat the word "R-h-i-o-c-e-r-h-o-s." He missed it by one letter. Tommy was the first one out of the game. Several boys laughed. That hurt, it hurt badly! Why did kids have to be so mean? Why?

sunnyside cafe

At last, it was lunch time. Tommy told himself everything would be better at lunch. Tommy walked along the lunch line and picked up his tray and looked in every direction hoping that just one kid would ask him to sit with them. No one did. He tried to be brave and took his tray to a table with only three boys but when he laid his tray down the boys scooted to make sure there was no room and said, "Our table is full!" Tommy sat at a table eating his lunch all by himself.

Tommy dreaded even thinking of going to recess after lunch. Tommy looked around the playground and saw some kids playing football, soccer, and basketball. Surely, somebody would ask him to play. If only one kid. He finally walked over to several games hoping somebody would ask if he wanted to play. No one did, no one! Finally, he sat down with his head hung low. He felt so alone, he hated this school! The kids were mean. He looked down and it was hard to hold the tears back. Just then, a boy came up to him and said, "Hi, my name is Ty Monroe. Can I sit beside you?" Tommy nodded as he looked up. The boy had a smile and he wore glasses too.

He told Tommy, "I am kind of new too. They used to pick on me too but now that you are here, they have kind of left me alone. I am really glad you are here Tommy." Just then the bell rang, and Tommy and Ty were the last two to go inside. The class started and they had a lot of math to do. Finally, the teacher said, "It is time to go to P.E." The gym teacher let them have a free play day. A bunch of boys formed around the basketball goal. Sean and Tim appointed themselves captains and kept taking turns and picking who they wanted to be on their team. There was only one boy left. The teacher saw what was happening and said, "Boys, I see exactly what you are doing, and this is not ok! You boys include Tommy right this minute! What are you boys thinking?"

At the end of the day, the bell rang, and it was finally time to go home. As he hurried out the classroom door, a boy knocked Tommy's books out of his hands. Tommy was not sure if the boy did it on purpose, or not but either way the boy did not stop to help him pick them up. He just kept going. Tommy was so embarrassed. Then he looked up and saw Ty bent over beside him helping him pick up his books. Tommy said behind the tears, "Thank you Ty, if only you were in my class! If only!

As they turned the corner to head toward their buses, Ty told Tommy that tomorrow would be better, but Tommy just shook his head and said, "I just don't want to be at this school." He had tears in his eyes. Tommy ran to catch his bus and saw an open seat in the back of the bus and quickly scooted all the way over by the window. A bit later a girl in his class sat beside him but she never said a word the whole way home. She did not even acknowledge him. Finally, the bus driver stopped in front of Tommy's house and Tommy hurried down the steps and ran into the house as fast as he could. He ran right past Aunt Bessie who was holding a plate of warm chocolate chip cookies at the front door.

Tommy ran to his bedroom and threw himself on the bed sobbing. It had been a terrible, horrible, awful day. He hugged his old, tattered bear. Why, why did he have to leave his family and then go to a brand-new school where the kids were so mean? Why? Aunt Bessie's heart broke to see Tommy on his bed sobbing. She tried to console him but nothing she said could make him stop crying. Aunt Bessie rubbed his back and kissed his head. She told him she wanted to hear what happened when he was ready to come to the kitchen to talk.

Finally, Tommy went to the kitchen and sat down. "Why do there have to be mean kids?" Aunt Bessie asked him what happened. Tommy told her all about Sam Stafford making fun of his glasses, about the kids not letting him play soccer because he was not good enough, how he and Ty were the last ones picked at basketball and only because the teacher made them, about how he stuttered and was the first one out at "Around the World" and two boys laughed, how on the bus no one would scoot over until the bus driver yelled at the kids to move over, and how the boy knocked his books out of his hands and didn't even help pick them up. He told her about having to eat lunch by himself. Aunt Bessie got tears in her eyes as she listened. She sat beside Tommy and patted his arms and said, "I am so sorry all this happened Tommy."

"You know what Tommy, tomorrow I am going up to school and make an appointment to see your teacher Mrs. Smith. I just know if she knew these things took place today, she would have put a stop to it. I know she would have dealt with those kids who were mean." That night Aunt Bessie and Uncle Bob talked a long time. They decided that Uncle Bob would take Tommy on a fishing and hiking adventure the next day while Aunt Bessie visited with the teacher.

As soon as class started that morning, a young boy knocked on Mrs. Smith's classroom door. The boy was Ty Monroe. Ty asked Ms. Smith if she could step outside; he had something important he needed tell her right away. Ty told Ms. Smith all about what the kids did to Tommy the day before. He told her about them laughing at his glasses, not letting him play soccer, no one wanting him on their basketball teams, about the boys snickering at him when he was the first out at "Around the World" and stuttering, how no one let him sit with them at lunch and how a boy knocked the books out of Tommy's hands and then laughed. Tears swelled up in Ms. Smith's eyes. She was mortified! "I am setting up a meeting with the principal right now! This kind of behavior must stop!!! Thank you, Ty for coming and telling me. Thank you for standing up for Tommy and doing the right thing, Ty. You are a good friend. We need more kids like you."

Aunt Bessie visited with Mrs. Smith on her plan time. Mrs. Smith said, "Oh I am so glad you are here. A student told me what happened to Tommy yesterday. I am just so sorry! I want you to know I have already told the principal, Mr. DoRight what happened to Tommy, and we are meeting with all the students right before lunch. Those students involved will have a consequence, and we are going to give all the students a lesson on how to treat other kids. Please tell Tommy this behavior will not be tolerated, and I am so sorry this all happened to him."

Uncle Bob and Tommy enjoyed the day together fishing and Uncle Bob told him he had a similar experience happen to him when he was a kid. He told Tommy that one day he was playing basketball and the kids saw he was good. One boy like Ty Monroe stepped out and said, "Hey, you are good! Can we play together?" He told Tommy because of that "ONE BOY" standing up and being his friend, his world changed. Uncle Bob said, "I think Ty Monroe is that boy at your school. I think you and Ty will be close friends. I know Bessie talked to Mrs. Smith and it will be better Tommy, I just know it."

After telling Mr. DoRight everything that had happened to Tommy, the principal came in the classroom and had everyone sit on the carpet and said, "Do you know why Tommy isn't at school today? Why would he want to come to school after a day like his first day of school? Why would he want to come after being left out, being made fun of, and laughed at? This is simply not acceptable at our school or anywhere to treat another student, especially a new student, like we have. I am so disappointed!!!" He then informed the students that if there were any further incidents like this, those students would have detention for at least three days. The kids who were guilty started to hang their heads. So what are we going to do to make this right? The awful things that were said and done hurt Tommy badly. Those words and actions cannot be erased but we are going to try to help him heal. I want you students to think how you would feel right this moment if all this happened to you. What can we possibly do or

Tommy

Please Don't Make
Fun of Me

Session II

Mrs. Smith asked the students the second time. "What can we possibly do or say to make Tommy feel better?" She waited for their reply. Jose' finally raised his hand and said, "We could ask him to play basketball with us." Another boy said, "We could pick Tommy first when we pick teams." Sally raised her hand and said, "I could ask Tommy if he would sit with me on the bus and if we could study our spelling words together." Another student replied, "We could save him a place to eat with us at lunch." Jackie Brown raised his hand and said, "We could cheer him on when we play "Around the World." Even Sam Stafford chimed in with, "I could tell Tommy he is a good speller and that I missed the same number he did, and I had a chance to see them." Johnny Rodrigues raised his hand and said, "I feel really bad for what I said and how I made Tommy feel yesterday. I am sorry we did those things to Tommy. If he comes tomorrow, I will ask him to be my friend."

When Tommy and Uncle Bob came home Aunt Bessie told Tommy what the principal had said. She also showed Tommy all the notes Mrs. Chronister brought that the students had written and told Tommy he should go and read them all. Tommy came out later with a big grin on his face. Aunt Bessie could tell he had been crying but this time the tears were of joy instead of hurt. He gave Aunt Bessie a big hug and she hugged him tight in return. Tommy heard the doorbell ring and Uncle Bob yelled that there was a young man at the door named Ty Monroe who wanted to see him. Tommy got a big smile on his face. He could not believe it! Ty had somehow found out where he lived. Tommy went to the door with a grin on his face. "How did you know where I live?" Tommy asked. Ty smiled big, "Well, I had to do some massive investigating! Actually, my mom helped me find your house. I just live a few blocks away.

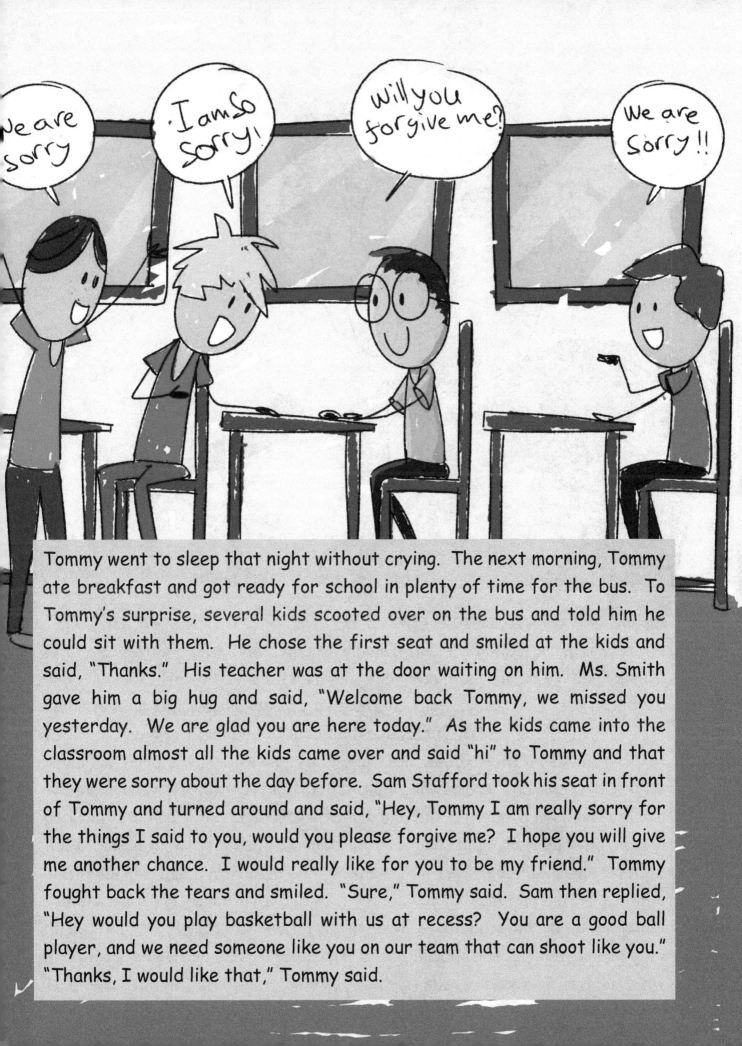

Tommy went to sleep that night without crying. The next morning, Tommy ate breakfast and got ready for school in plenty of time for the bus. To Tommy's surprise, several kids scooted over on the bus and told him he could sit with them. He chose the first seat and smiled at the kids and said, "Thanks." His teacher was at the door waiting on him. Ms. Smith gave him a big hug and said, "Welcome back Tommy, we missed you yesterday. We are glad you are here today." As the kids came into the classroom almost all the kids came over and said "hi" to Tommy and that they were sorry about the day before. Sam Stafford took his seat in front of Tommy and turned around and said, "Hey, Tommy I am really sorry for the things I said to you, would you please forgive me? I hope you will give me another chance. I would really like for you to be my friend." Tommy fought back the tears and smiled. "Sure," Tommy said. Sam then replied, "Hey would you play basketball with us at recess? You are a good ball player, and we need someone like you on our team that can shoot like you." "Thanks, I would like that," Tommy said.

At recess, Sam called Ty and Tommy's names and said, "Our team gets Tommy and Ty on our side, and they play first instead of me." Tommy and Ty had a great time and right at the end of recess saw Mr. DoRight and Mrs. Smith at the end of the basketball court cheering them all on. They had big smiles on their faces. At the end of two weeks, the principal came on the intercom and said to the whole school. "Attention! Attention please! Good afternoon students, this morning the teachers and I had a meeting and we have all seen a big change in our school these last two weeks. What a difference "Random Acts of Kindness" has made! We are implementing a new program and making our school a School of Character! Now we are going to need two student leaders to be on our Character Committee to help promote ideas for showing good character. We need you students to vote for two Sunnyside students that you think would be the best leaders."

On Monday morning, Mr. James came back on the intercom to announce who the two kids for outstanding leadership at Sunnyside Elementary would be. He cleared his throat and announced. "The two students who got an overwhelming number of votes to represent our students at our school goes to...... Mr. Tommy Allbright and Mr. Ty Monroe!!!! I personally couldn't be more pleased with your votes students. Tommy and Ty will be our outstanding Leaders of Tomorrow! Congratulations Ty and Tommy."

Tommy and Ty continued to be friends; actually, they were friends with everyone. That is why all the kids at Sunnyside liked them. Tommy and Ty formed a "Welcome Team" and every new student that came to Sunnyside school had a buddy and several students assigned to show them around the first few days until they felt comfortable on their own. Tommy and Ty did a great job being Leaders of Tomorrow. The local TV station wanted to do a special report on the Sunnyside Elementary Character Program. The report was put on TV and all the newspapers. The school keeps the newspaper articles on the hallway bulletin board at the school and the Leaders of Tomorrow program is still in action today. Because of ONE STUDENT who befriended Tommy and stood up for Tommy, his world changed forever! Tommy and Ty remained best friends throughout Junior High and High School. As an adult, Tommy Allbright traveled all over the country speaking to elementary schools teaching kids to speak up for someone who is being picked on. He never forgot his friend, Ty Monroe, who changed his world.

I hope you are a Ty Monroe! It will change a student's life and your life too!

Acknowledgements

A special thank you to my readers Marge Frantz and Sally Bowman. Thank you to my friend and neighbor, Mike Webb who helped me so much in formatting this book. Also, to Jamie Fleming, school librarian for helping me with last minute deadline issues. Lastly, a huge "thank you" to my incredible husband, Ken. His constant encouragement and his help taking care of the house so I could work on this book. I couldn't have done this book without these people. I am forever grateful.

Follow Up Discussion Questions

1) How do you think Tommy felt when he had to leave his home and move in with his aunt and uncle he never knew before he got to Oklahoma?

2) Why do you think he was so scared to go to a new school? What did he worry about?

3) List the ways the students were cruel to Tommy on that first day of school?

4) How do you think Tommy felt at the end of that first day of school?

   (Suggestion: Tear out the picture of Tommy on the next
   page. Each time a child describes how Tommy felt, (hurt, bruised,
   scarred, ripped apart, torn, crushed, etc.) wad up a corner of the
   paper a bit each time a word is spoken to describe Tommy's
   feelings.) By this time, Tommy looks like a paper wad and must feel like
   trash. Let children express how hurt he must feel.

5) Ask children what does Tommy need?

   (Emphasize: A friend, someone to play with, to be included, someone to sit with
   at lunch, for someone to scoot over on the bus, to be picked for the
   basketball team, to be noticed, for students to be kind etc....

6) Will Tommy always remember these hurtful words and actions?

   Suggestion: Try to flatten the picture of Tommy. Hold it up. Does Tommy
   look like he did the first morning when he felt so good about
   himself? Explain: Tommy is bruised, hurt, scarred, broken,
   and maybe difficult for him to trust other kids after this.

7) Even though Tommy forgave the ugly words and deeds, they can never be taken away.
   The scars will always be in the back of his mind.

   Suggestion: May use two experiments with students at this time.

   Experiment 1)
   Call a student up and put a strip of toothpaste on his/her finger.
   Give the student 30 seconds to put the toothpaste back into the tube perfectly
   without a mess. (It is not possible to do.)
   Discuss: Once ugly words are spoken, the words can't be erased as if
   they were never said, but you can say you are sorry and apologize.

   Experiment 2)
   Teacher holds up a clear glass of water, teacher has a student
   put one spoonful of dirt into glass of water each time teacher gives an example
   of hurtful things she has heard said in her classroom. By the end of six or
   seven examples, the student stirs the glass of water and now it is extremely
   dirty. Like a student who comes to school happy and feeling good in the
   morning can quickly be made to feel ugly and dirty by students who say and do mean
   things.

8) Did Tommy do the right thing to forgive? **Discuss:** It is important to forgive. It frees us.

9) Who turned Tommy's life around and brighten his day? What kind of young man was Ty Monroe?

10) What are some things you can do for a new student or any student that may be hurting?

11) Should we stand up for someone who is being made fun of?

12) Who do we go tell if mean kids do not stop?

   Example: teacher, counselor, principal, parents etc...

13) Can one student make a difference?

14) That did Ty and Tommy do to make a BIG impact in Sunnyside Elementary?

Don't Make Fun of Me

Don't laugh and make fun of me
I have feelings too why can't you see
No one wants to be called hurtful names
Can't you look inside and see my pain.

Don't leave me out when you pick kids for your games
Don't you know how bad it hurts when you never call my name
I hear your laughs and snickers when you think I don't hear
I see all your actions; you make it quite clear.

I may wear thick glasses and my teeth have braces
Don't you know all kids have feelings behind those sad faces
Some say words don't hurt like sticks and stones
I will tell you; your words hurt to my heart and my bones.

Some are born different like in this wheelchair
It hurts when people point, whisper and stare
Instead, you could talk to me and show me you care
That would make me feel special but that is kind of rare.

Would you be the one who stands up for the kid in pain
You would be a leader and have a new friendship to gain
I hope you will be the one who will stand up and be kind
Kids like you are the ones we all want to find.

So, from today on, I want my kindness to show
I want everyone to feel wanted and special this I know
I pledge to do my best to show all kids love
It is what our world needs a lot more of.

Rachel Chronister
Counselor

CPSIA information can be obtained
at www.ICGtesting.com
Printed in the USA
BVHW011256231121
PP12873300001B/1

9 781737 985105